HOTEL TRANSYLVANIA
THE SERIES

BAT FLAP FEVER!

Adapted by Ximena Hastings
Based on the screenplay written by Ben Joseph

Ready-to-Read

Simon Spotlight

New York   London   Toronto   Sydney   New Delhi

SIMON SPOTLIGHT
An imprint of Simon & Schuster Children's Publishing Division
1230 Avenue of the Americas, New York, New York 10020
This Simon Spotlight edition August 2020
TM & © 2020 Sony Pictures Animation Inc. All Rights Reserved.
For information about special discounts for bulk purchases, please contact
Simon & Schuster Special Sales at 1-866-506-1949 or business@simonandschuster.com.
Manufactured in the United States of America 0720 LAK
10 9 8 7 6 5 4 3 2 1
ISBN 978-1-5344-7111-5 (hc)
ISBN 978-1-5344-7110-8 (pbk)
ISBN 978-1-5344-7112-2 (eBook)

Mavis is chatting with
her friends when she gets
a special letter from her dad,
Dracula.

"My dearest Mavis," the letter starts, "I just wanted to tell you that I finally created a *cool* new product! And since you are the *coolest* vampire I know, I am naming it after you!"

"I am sending it over now, so get
ready for the Mavey-Waveys!"
the letter finishes.

Mavis opens up the box. She can't
wait to see the product named
after her!

When Mavis finishes unpacking the
box, she pulls out . . . a bat costume!
Mavis's friends laugh.
"Those are the *cool* Mavey-Waveys?"
Pedro asks. "They look more like
Mavey-*Lameys*!"

But Mavis doesn't think the wings
are lame.
To prove that they *are* cool,
she tries them on.

Her friends laugh even more once they are on. Even Aunt Lydia and Diane the Chicken think it's funny. "I don't care what anyone says. I'm going to rock these wings!" Mavis says proudly.

Mavis walks around the hotel,
showing off her new
Mavey-Waveys. She thinks they are
super cool . . . that is, until even
easy tasks start to become difficult.

First, Mavis realizes she can't take the wings off, so she has to eat her favorite burger without using her hands!
Then she has trouble walking around without knocking everything down!

Mavis heads to her room.
"These wings aren't cool!"
she admits.
She tosses them out of her window.
"Now everything can go back to
normal," Mavis says.

What Mavis doesn't know is that things do *not* go back to normal. The wings fly away and land at Mr. Cartwright's house.

When Mavis leaves her room and goes down to the lobby, all the monsters are hysterical. The hotel is on lockdown!

"Dad? What is going on?" Mavis asks. Her dad is using the Vampire Council Emergency Crystal Ball to warn her.

"The humans broke into the
hotel when we were sleeping and
stole the Mavey-Waveys!"
Aunt Lydia tells them.

Mavis pretends to act surprised.
She doesn't know how to tell her
dad that this is all her fault!

But Mavis has a plan to get
the wings back.

Mavis sneaks away while the other monsters watch the humans on a TV screen.

Mr. Cartwright is just playing with his daughter, but Quasi thinks otherwise.

"The humans want to use the wings to destroy us!" Quasi shouts.

Meanwhile, Mavis creeps over to
the Cartwrights' backyard.
Her plan is to take the wings
and hurry back home to Hotel
Transylvania.

As soon as Mavis reaches for the wings, Mrs. Cartwright appears! Mavis transforms herself into a bat to disguise herself. She hides behind the Cartwrights' baby.

"This is not good," Mavis whispers
to herself. "I have to get out of here."
Mavis starts flapping her real bat
wings to get away, but she's
carrying the baby, too!

Mavis lets go of the baby, and
Mr. Cartwright catches her safely.
But he still has the Mavey-Waveys!
There's only one thing left for Mavis
to do.

When Mavis gets back to the hotel, she confesses to her dad.

"This is really hard to admit, but this is kind of my fault. I'm sorry, Dad," Mavis says. "I really, really tried to like the wings, but they were just so silly. I *kind* of threw them out the window."

Dracula is a little disappointed in Mavis, but he doesn't tell anyone else what she did.

"Listen up, monsters," Dracula
announces.
"We really don't need to fight the
humans. The wings are right here!"
Dracula makes shadow wings with
his hands.

He can't fool Aunt Lydia, though. "What did Mavis say to you?" she asks.

"Mavis just said Dracula is the
coolest monster around!
Right, Mavey-Wavey?"
Dracula asks.
Mavis groans but agrees.
"Yes, you are *super cool*, Dad."

"Great! The lockdown is officially over!" Dracula exclaims.
Mavis and Dracula head back to the lobby together.

"Mavey, I'm sorry I made you wear those wings," Dracula says. "Never forget you can always talk to me about anything."

"I know. That's what makes you *super cool*. I'm sorry," Mavis responds.

"I am glad you think I am super cool," Dracula says before leaving, "because there's another product coming your way soon . . . it's the Mavey-*Savey*!"